DON'T RETIRE

—

RENEW

The New Concept of Life
After Work

Live Life To Its Fullest In
Renewalment

BY LOU KAUFMANN

WWW.RENEWALMENT.COM

Trafford
PUBLISHING

Order this book online at www.trafford.com/08-0657
or email orders@trafford.com

Most Trafford titles are also available at major online book retailers.

Note for Librarians: A cataloguing record for this book is available from Library
and Archives Canada at www.collectionscanada.ca/amicus/index-e.html

Printed in Victoria, BC, Canada.

ISBN: 978-1-4251-7906-9

*We at Trafford believe that it is the responsibility of us all, as both individuals
and corporations, to make choices that are environmentally and socially sound.
You, in turn, are supporting this responsible conduct each time you purchase a
Trafford book, or make use of our publishing services. To find out how you are
helping, please visit www.trafford.com/responsiblepublishing.html*

*Our mission is to efficiently provide the world's finest, most comprehensive
book publishing service, enabling every author to experience success.
To find out how to publish your book, your way, and have it available
worldwide, visit us online at www.trafford.com/10510*

 www.trafford.com

North America & international
toll-free: 1 888 232 4444 (USA & Canada)
phone: 250 383 6864 ♦ fax: 250 383 6804 ♦ email: info@trafford.com

The United Kingdom & Europe
phone: +44 (0)1865 722 113 ♦ local rate: 0845 230 9601
facsimile: +44 (0)1865 722 868 ♦ email: info.uk@trafford.com

10 9 8 7 6 5 4 3 2

DEDICATION

I dedicate this work of love to my wife Judy. She inspired me when she had planned to retire and the ideas for the book began at that moment. She continues to be an inspiration to me in our daily lives with her positive attitudes about all that we are confronted with every day.

Her help with ideas, and the editing of this book are Fantastic and I could not have done this without her.

CONTENTS

WWW.RENEWALMENT.COM

INTRODUCTION

This book was written based on certain facts already established. One, that you are at the age where you have decided to retire or stop working at the job that you have had for many years. Second, your retirement income is such that at least you know that your current bills and obligations can be met. Third, that your health, although not what it was when you were younger, has not crippled you.

And lastly, that your overall attitude is such that as you have reached this point in your life, you are open to new ideas and suggestions and possible changes that may affect your life.

This book is not written with any political philosophy or ways to change global warming or improve the world. It is written to improve your life and that of your spouse or those you love. It is written to be used as a "daily" message, one that we follow one day at a time. There is an old adage that "if you steal one idea it is plagiarism, if you steal many ideas, it is research." I have tried to do my research for this book.

For the purposes of this book, it is about 74 years of a life lived, plus many read books, magazine articles, newspapers gleaned over and a view of the world today through friends and television.

Please take these ideas, concepts and thoughts and put them to work in your daily life, see if you can't live a total new life of "Renewalment."

ABOUT LOU KAUFMANN

Lou Kaufmann, now in his seventies, is in Semi-Renewalment and still active as a Real Estate Broker for his company, ERA Kaufmann Associates, in Bella Vista, Arkansas. Lou has been in the real estate business over thirty years.

Lou has had an outstanding career in the sales profession since the time he was discharged from the U.S. Air Force. He sold life insurance in New Jersey and became an Account Executive for NBC TV in Las Vegas, Nevada in 1960. He later became associated with Success Motivation Institute, sold Success and trained and motivated many of the leading companies in Las Vegas at that time.

Lou became District Manager with Midas Mufflers in 1973 and eventually became Vice President of the Midas dealership in El Paso, Texas. He received his real estate license in El Paso and became Marketing Director for Meca Homes. He sold or caused to be sold over 400 homes in a five year period and opened up his own real estate company, eventually being recruited to Northwest Arkansas and opening his own office in Bella Vista.

Lou is proud of his involvement with the U.S. Jaycees and of his achievements in that organization. He is the Former State President of the Nevada Jaycees, he is a former Vice President of the U.S. Jaycees and was a candidate for

President of the U.S. Jaycees. He was nominated as an Outstanding Young Man in 1967 in Las Vegas, Nevada and served as Chairman of the Governors Council on Physical Fitness, named by Governor Paul Laxalt. Lou is the former President of the El Paso Kiwanis Club, the Las Cruces Cancer Association and as a licensed pilot, President of the El Paso Aviation Association. He has an honorable discharge from both the U.S. Navy and the U.S. Air Force and attended Monmouth University in Long Branch, New Jersey.

Lou and his lovely wife of three years, Judy, live in Semi-Renewalment in Bella Vista, Arkansas.

CHAPTER I

RENEWALMENT CAN BE WONDERFUL OR SAD

Retirement can be something wonderful or it can be sad. It can be the beginning of a new phase in your life or it can be the end of a great or mediocre career.

In April 2006, my wife, who at that time was an accountant for a local public accounting firm, had decided she would retire at the end of tax season on April 15th. She had been a CPA in Texas for many years. When she moved to Arkansas, she decided to work as an accountant. We had discussed her retirement and how she could then work with me in the real estate business handling all the financial aspects of our company.

She came home the night of April 14th, crying. I asked her what the problem was and she just said that the idea of leaving the accounting business in the manner that she knew was leaving her sad. She had been doing this for some thirty years and did enjoy her career. I told her that she really wasn't retiring but starting a new career working with me in real estate. The word retirement caused her great anguish as if it was the end instead of going in a new direction.

As we talked about it over our cocktails, it dawned on me that it was the word "retirement" that was causing her great concern. We then decided we needed to come up with a different word that was more positive and upbeat, one that could have the same meaning but still give direction toward the intent.

We mentioned a few words and then came to the word "renew" and I went to the Webster's Dictionary and looked up the word. Right off the bat, it came at us immediately that it was a tremendous word to use as a replacement and from that moment on she went into "renewalment". According to Webster, renew means "to begin or take up again, to restore or replenish, to revive, re-establish, make new as if new again, to be restored to a former state."

Renewal means, "The act of renewing."

We then looked up the words retire and retirement in Webster's Dictionary. Retire means "to withdraw or go away, to a place of abode, shelter or seclusion, to fall back or retreat in an orderly fashion and according to plan, as from battle." And retirement means "withdrawal into privacy or seclusion."

It was at that point and at that moment in our lives that we immediately replaced "retirement" with "renewalment" and began to look at life after work in a totally different way. Our definition of "renewalment" is "when one career ends and you decide to renew your life in a new and exciting direction."

As a young executive many years ago, (I am now 74 years old), and a former Vice President of the U.S. Jaycees, I traveled around and gave many speeches and motivational talks to various type of groups. At one such speech I had said how many people in the post office set a goal to retire at the first chance they get, and having no further goals to work toward, retire and within a year they die. The Postmaster of the El Paso, Texas post office came up to me after the meeting and said how accurate I was and how sad it was that so many of his friends who had worked many years at the post office, decided to retire and within that year after retiring, had passed away.

Knowing today that this happens so very often, we decided to change the word and the concept of retirement and give it new meaning for ourselves and for any of our friends and others who would like to share in this new approach to life after life. It has given us hope, excitement, new goals and a wonderful way to continue our lives together.

As we talk, plan and have fun with our new concept of life, many new ideas come into focus. At the age of 72 I had planned to retire on December 15, 2006, but with renewalment, that goal went out the window. It was replaced with the idea that I would go into "semi-renewalment", which we defined as "continuing to work but take our leisure time whenever we want."

The idea of renewalment gave us a whole new outlook on how we would spend the rest of our lives. We can look at many of the things we do in a totally new way when our lives take on a positive approach to all you do when you renew and begin over.

Isn't it great to start life over when you decide to and not when someone determines that you "need to go into seclusion." Retirement is an arbitrary requirement that started with the Kaiser in Germany, prior to World War I, who decided that age 65 was the right age for people in his country to retire. That concept was initiated in the United States not long after and pretty much became the mandatory age for people to quit working.

Airline pilots must retire at age 60, just at a time when they have gained all that experience that we depend on so much. The idea of retirement is constantly bantered about and many companies force top executives and middle management out, at a point in their lives when their knowledge is at the greatest.

One of the biggest concerns for all those close to retirement is certainly financial and of course, their long term health situation. Without an adequate income, how will they be able to survive in their retirement years? Certainly Social Security is not enough.

This book is created to help all people look at life after retirement in a different way and not be afraid of it. It is written so that you can totally renew your life at an age where we stop one career and begin another. It helps you to have plans to go in a totally new and renewed direction with your change of work status in your senior years. It helps you to live happy, successful, productive lives until the time our God calls us.

CHAPTER 2

SUCCESS AT ANY AGE

What is Success? How do you define it? What does Success mean to you? Is everyone interested in success? According to Webster's dictionary, success means "the favorable or prosperous termination of attempts or endeavors." "The attainment of wealth, position and honors." But success to many people has other definitions. If you ask someone what success means to them, as many people as you ask, you can have that many definitions. Success can be becoming a millionaire, or achieving a certain position within a company or starting your own business or whatever you want it to be. It could be a happy marriage, a wonderful family, excellent health, a nice home, any one of them or all of them.

Many years ago, Andrew Carnegie, the great steel magnate, was looking for a person to write a book about success. He planned to give the individual who would take the time to do the research and compile the information into a book, introductions to one hundred of the most famous people of that time--people he knew and had a friendship or acquaintance with. People like John D. Rockefeller, Thomas Edison, and Henry Ford to name a few. The writer was to interview them and find out how they became successful. What did they do to achieve the success they attained?

He interviewed Napoleon Hill, a young man at that time, and said he would give him the introductions but would not pay him to do the job. The candidate would have to sustain himself. Unbeknown to Napoleon Hill, Carnegie had a stop watch in his hand and was only going to give him sixty seconds to make a decision. Hill did not have to think about it. He said he would do it. After interviewing all those great people of that era, Hill wrote a book called Laws of Success which he later shortened to Think and Grow Rich, one of the all time best self help books and still popular today.

What Napoleon Hill found when he interviewed all those successful people, the common thread that wound through all of them, the one common bond they all had was, "Success is the Progressive Realization of Worthwhile, Predetermined, Personal Goals." That was it! They all had their individual goals and a plan to achieve them. Different goals, different plans, different people, but goals to take them in the direction they wanted to go.

"Progressive". To me, this is one of the most important elements of the definition of success. It is ongoing, never ending. It doesn't stop when you "retire". Like the energizer bunny, it goes on and on and on. If you understand success and the importance of goal setting, you will do it the rest of your life. Napoleon Hill became very successful. He was wealthy, an advisor to Presidents, author of many books on success and speaker at many seminars around the world. When he reached age 65, he certainly could have retired comfortably and lived happily ever after. But when he died around the age of 87, they found in his personal effects, a plan of action and goals that would have taken him to the age of 107. Henry Ford, a very goal directed individual had a plan of action and goals that would have taken him to the age of 127. Oddly enough, the majority of people in this country have no goals whatsoever.

Statistics used by the insurance industry and many other types of business will tell you that only three percent of the population have any true understanding of what they want to do with their life. These are the successful ones as they have their goals written down and defined with a plan of action to achieve them. Ten percent of the population work hard toward success, are working on their plan, trying to get their goals in the proper perspective, but have not yet achieved the ultimate success. Fifty percent of our population have no goals. They get up in the morning, go to work, come home at night, have dinner, watch television, go to bed, and then do it all over again. Thirty seven percent of the population have no idea what is happening to them. They are carrying their umbilical cord looking for a place to plug into. Welfare, government subsidy, a free lunch, and you know, there ain't no such thing as a "free lunch."

"Realization." As you study how to set and establish goals, you need to have goals that are obtainable. Some are a long way off, some are next week, some are hard,

16

some are easy, and you don't ever want to set goals so unobtainable that your success is only an illusion. You must realize victories along the way. A small weight loss, an increase in income, a move in the right direction toward your goals. You know what they say, "Yard by yard it is hard, but inch by inch it is a cinch."

"Worthwhile." Your goals must have value. They cannot be illegal, immoral or hurt other people. They must be "Predetermined." You start planning today for tomorrow, next week, next month, next year, your life. There are short term goals and long term goals. There are tangible goals and intangible goals. Knowing the difference and how you fit into those circumstances will determine the outcome of your success. Your goals are "Personal." They are yours. Not your wife's, not your boss's, not someone else's, but yours. You can share them or not. Someone can be a part of yours or not, but in the long run, these are your goals and your plans and you are the one who will work on them and achieve the success.

Going back to Webster's definition of success, it stated, "the favorable or prosperous termination of attempts or endeavors." One very important thing to know about success and truly to understand is, it is not when you achieve your goals that you become successful, it is when you are "working" on your goals that you are successful. Remember, Success is a Journey, it is not a Destination.

CHAPTER 3

DEFINING THE AREAS
OF YOUR LIFE

Where do you start when you're setting goals? Can you begin setting goals at age 50, 60, in your seventies? Shouldn't I have started this when I was younger and had the physical stamina to work on them? Goals can be set at any age at any time. The goals change, the desires change, the energy levels change. But once you understand the goal setting process, you can establish goals at any time in your life, no matter your current situation. Whenever you are ready to make something positive happen in your life is the time for goal setting. Goal setting is fun. It is exciting. It gives you direction and it can give meaning and purpose to your life no matter where you are at the present time.

I went over to the coffee shop next to our office the other day where a gentleman was standing waiting for someone and I said "Hi". He said "Hello" and asked me how I was doing. I gave him my standard answer. "Fantastic" I said. We chatted briefly and I said I was still working and he responded, "I'm retired. No, I'm retarded". I thought about his "retarded" statement for awhile and thought what a shame he thought that way because I know when he feeds that into his "computer" that type of thinking is what comes out.

18

When you get into the Renewal stage of your life and begin setting new goals and get rid of the "stinking thinking", a whole new environment and vista opens up to you. Many people, no matter their age in life, never get to set goals because they don't know where to begin. They haven't taken an evaluation of themselves to determine their assets and liabilities, their strong and weak points to or determine just where they are now right now. Are they where they want to be in their life at this point in time? If not, where do they start? That's easy; you always start at the beginning.

If you don't know the questions to ask yourself, then at the end of this chapter you will find a series of questions you can answer "yes" or "no". By your answer, you will determine if this area is important to you and whether it fits into your life at this time. If it is an area that is important to you then you need to mark that question as one where you may want to start setting some goals. There are so many factors to consider when you begin setting goals.

First of all, there are six areas of our lives we are concerned about and that is all there is. They are Family, Financial, Physical, Social, Mental and Spiritual. These are broken down into tangible and intangible goals and short range and long range goals. Now as you try to sort these out, it starts to get a little more involved and a little more complicated. This is the very reason that when you work on your goals, you always want to use a pencil with an eraser and begin writing everything down.

Writing is very integral to this whole process. You need to have a pad and pencil and begin writing your thoughts down. Writing develops the thought, the thought develops the plan and the plan develops the action to help you achieve your goals. Once you determine the goal, there is an orderly process that helps you develop the plan of action to achieve that goal.

First, you have to be specific in how you state the goal. It has to be legal, ethical, personal and morally right. You need to have a specific date when you plan on achieving the goal. You can't leave the date open or no date at all; this is why you have an eraser on your pencil. As you get closer to the date to achieve your goal and you are not where you think you should be, you can change the date or even start asking some very important questions of yourself regarding your goal.

Once your date is written down you then need to ask yourself, "If this is my goal, what is stopping me from achieving this goal?" What are the obstacles? You know what is keeping you from achieving any goal that you set. It might be money, time, education, desire, other people, energy level, or what you are really willing to give up or really willing to work hard at. Once you know what the obstacles are, and you will know them when you write them down, now it is a matter to come up with the solutions. Start writing them down. For every obstacle, there could be ten solutions. If you have ten obstacles, you could have 100 solutions. With that many areas to work on, you could be overwhelmed and begin to feel that it wasn't a good goal or that you didn't want to work that hard. This is when you ask yourself the all important question. Look at the solutions and ask, "Is it worth it to me?" If the answer is yes, you have yourself a good goal. If the answer is no, forget it and move on.

In addition to the evaluation questionnaire, we will give you some examples of how to write out your goals and develop the plan to get you where you want to go.

The first part of the program is to evaluate your current Financial situation to see how your Renewalment years are going to work out. There are so many situations today where people who have set a goal to renew and then because of the current housing market slump, stocks taking a nose dive or gas prices going up dramatically, their investment program has left them in a situation where they decide they are going to delay renewalment for a few more years.

When you look at your total income from your pensions, IRA's, social security, is it enough to take care of all your necessary needs? Even though you have planned to do this for a long time, when you get there, it's not that easy or what you expected. Maybe you have no choice but to renew because of the job you were in, or age factors or the company merged and changes were made that didn't take you into account. Regardless, you are now renewed.

If your income is not enough to allow you to renew as comfortably as you had thought, you may want to go into Semi-renewalment. This is a state where you might do some part time work, or consulting, or write a book or be creative and come up with new ideas for you to make additional income. Go ahead now and evaluate yourself in your Financial area and at the end, if you need a few ideas to make additional income, we will suggest a few.

YOUR GOAL SETTING PLAN OF ACTION
SELF EVALUATION

In establishing goals for yourself at this time of your life, it is important to understand your current assets and liabilities. This is not necessarily in the meaning of dollars and cents; this is about your current life and what some of your weak areas might be and certainly your strong points. Following are questions that need to be answered, either yes or no. If you answer no on a question this might be an area that you would like to strengthen and where some specific goals could be set. Even a yes answer might be an area that you might want to establish certain new goals.

These questions are only meant to be a stimulus and to give you ideas to further help you to stimulate your thoughts and actions. Understand, no one is going to see this so be honest with yourself. These are your personal goals and only you are aware of what you really want and need.

FINANCIAL EVALUATION

1. Do you have a definite goal for your Renewalment Years? **Yes No**

2. Have you set Time Limits to reach those goals? **Yes No**

3. Do you give Financial Development at this time in your life proper planning? **Yes No**

4. Are you sincerely working with others to reach your goals? **Yes No**

5. Have you planned for your Financial Future up to this point in your life? **Yes No**

6. Are you still working? **Yes No**

7. Do you want to work or do something that would assist you financially? **Yes No**

8. Do you plan your time daily? **Yes No**

9. Do you diligently work your plan? **Yes No**

10. If you are still working, do you constantly search out ways you can improve your job? **Yes No**

11. Do you always do your homework? **Yes No**

12. Are you up to date on current developments in your field?   **Yes No**

13. If you had your own business, could you work effectively and productively alone?   **Yes No**

14. Would you like to have a home based business at this time?   **Yes No**

15. Do you have an operating budget at this stage in your life?   **Yes No**

16. Do you spend money wisely?   **Yes No**

17. Do you still save regularly?   **Yes No**

18. Do have an investment program?   **Yes No**

19. Is what you save adequate?   **Yes No**

20. If you had to at this time in your life, could you increase your financial worth and assets in the next twelve months?   **Yes No**

21. How much would you like to earn in the next 12 months? $_____.

22. Are you currently living within your financial means?   **Yes No**

23. At this point in your life, do you have a sufficient insurance program? **Yes No**

24. Do you have a good credit rating? **Yes No**

25. Is having a good credit rating important to you at this point in your life? **Yes No**

26. Do have an up to date financial statement? **Yes No**

27. Are your savings adequate to carry you for the next twelve months? **Yes No**

28. Do you have a Will? **Yes No**

29. Do you have a plan for long term care if you needed it? **Yes No**

ADDITIONAL INCOME IDEAS IN RENEWALMENT

Consulting – Taking your years of experience in your previous work and offering your services to a business that may require it.

1. Seminars – Again, taking that experience and putting together a Seminar that you can offer to the public for a fee. One or two a month could give those extra dollars you need.

2. Internet – Establish a website. Sell a product. Sell a service. Many people never leave their home anymore and make lots of money using only their computer.

3. E-Bay – Learn how the program works and sell your stuff in your garage, your neighbor's garage, the block's garage. Somebody will buy it.

4. Write a book – With your years of experience, sit down and write it out and find a market for it, just as I have done.

5. Write magazine articles – There are hundreds and hundreds of magazines in this country that look for articles on their type of interest. I have some friends in Colorado, husband and wife, in renewalment, who do this all the time and support themselves.

6. Part time work – Be a Wal-Mart Greeter, or work in a Fast Food Restaurant. Many businesses prefer mature, senior citizens on whom they can rely and don't have to pay a lot of money.

7. Start a new business out of your home.

8. Get into Network Marketing with a good product and just mess around with it part time. Expand it, build it, and get others to do the work.

9. Get your Master Mind Group together and see what else you can do.

FAMILY PLANNING

As we plan around our Family situation, it is a lot different today than it was when we first got started as a family. The kids are gone and it is just the spouse and you. If you are like me, you may have lost a spouse or two and re-married or perhaps had a divorce or two and have started over again. Then again, at this time in your life, you may be single, for whatever reason.

If you are married, then you need to answer these questions as truthfully as you can. After you have answered these questions, you can have your spouse go over your answers and see if they agree. If not, there is room for discussion. These are not all the questions there are, but it is a beginning. I have tried to put some questions in for the single person so that they might evaluate their situation.

I don't know about you but I love a marriage with no arguments or disagreements and lots of excellent communication combined with lots of love. Is that possible? You bet your sweet bippy it is!

FAMILY EVALUATION

1. Do you spend enough time (quality time) alone with your spouse?   **Yes** **No**

2. Should you plan dinners out more often?   **Yes** **No**

3. Are family disagreements/arguments a problem?
                                                            Yes **No**

4. Can these problems be resolved?   **Yes** **No**

5. Do you feel that you communicate well with your spouse?   **Yes** **No**

6. Do you make the effort to express love to your Spouse?   **Yes** **No**

7. Is your family/spouse your priority and great importance in your life?   **Yes** **No**

8. Do you spend as much meaningful time together as possible?   **Yes** **No**

9. Are you and your spouse happy where you live?
                                                            Yes **No**

10. Do you have an up to date will drawn in case of unexpected death?   **Yes** **No**

11. Is communicating well with others one of your qualities? **Yes No**

12. Are family recreation times planned ahead? **Yes   No**

13. Are family vacations planned by you and your spouse? **Yes No**

14. Are family members health needs adequately cared for? **Yes No**

15. Do members of your family awake in the morning with a good positive attitude? **Yes No**

16. Is your family lifestyle what you want it to be? **Yes No**

17. Are you satisfied with your sex life with your spouse or could it be better at this point in your life? **Yes No**

18. Do you tell your spouse you love him/her often? **Yes No**

19. If single, do you wish you that you weren't? **Yes   No**

20. Do you have a plan to meet people and improve your situation? **Yes No**

HEALTH & PHYSICAL PLANNING

As we age, our body changes. Sometimes we are ok and sometimes we're not. You probably remember the old adage, "If I knew I was going to live this long I would have taken better care of myself." I would imagine most of us are guilty of that in our lives. How do you feel now? Is your weight ok or do you need to lose some? Have you given up smoking? Just a cocktail in the evening and not over doing it?

Are you exercising or just don't have time or take time? Have you been to the doctor lately for a check up or just think you don't need to go until you have a pain? Whatever physical problems you do have, do you have a plan to take care of them?

The whole idea of the following questions is to give you a current idea of just how you need to be thinking of one of the most important parts of your life right now. What a waste to get this far and then not be able to enjoy it.

You know what they say, "proper planning prevents p__s poor performance." So start planning on your Health. Feel Good, Look Good, Be Good and Good is what you are going to be.

KNOWING YOUR HEALTH

1. Are you in good health at the present time? **Yes** **No**

2. Is good health important to you at this time in your life? **Yes** **No**

3. Are your physical habits in line with good health? **Yes** **No**

4. Have you seen a doctor lately? **Yes** **No**

5. Have you been to the dentist lately? **Yes** **No**

6. Do you need to see an eye doctor? **Yes** **No**

7. If you smoke, would you like to quit smoking? **Yes** **No**

8. Are you overweight? **Yes** **No**

9. Would you like to lose weight? **Yes** **No**

10. Have you had a complete physical checkup in the last year? **Yes** **No**

11. Are you aware of the danger signs of major illnesses such as heart problems or cancer? **Yes** **No**

12. Do you get enough physical exercise? **Yes** **No**

13. Do you eat a proper diet?   **Yes**   **No**

14. Do you take vitamins?   **Yes**   **No**

15. Have you set goals for yourself for recreation and relaxing?   **Yes**   **No**

16. Do you exercise regularly?   **Yes**   **No**

17. Can you set up an exercise program for yourself?
                                                 Yes   **No**

18. Do you get enough hours of sleep?   **Yes**   **No**

19. Are your attitudes toward your health in the best interests of your family?   **Yes**   **No**

20. Would you like to play golf more often? Tennis?
                                                 Yes   **No**

HOW'S YOUR FAITH LEVEL TODAY

As you have reached your Renewalment age, spiritual thoughts and ideas may always have been a part of your life or it may not have been that important. Regardless, at this time in our lives we tend to think more about the end than we do the beginning. So the question is, do you believe or what do you believe in or does it matter at all to you?

Trust me, you need to believe in something that will give you fulfillment at this point in your life.

My wife and I are Christians and we believe in God and Jesus Christ. Over the years I have questioned many things about what I heard, read and observed but it all boils down to the Faith that you establish.

One of the lines of the Jaycee Creed states, "Faith in God gives meaning and purpose to human life." So ask yourself this question, what is your purpose in life?

As you go over the questions on your Spiritual Development, give serious thought to your answers. Judy and I start each day off with prayer and we have a strong belief in God that helps us to "enjoy every luscious moment." We want you to find that luscious moment every day that you and your loved ones can enjoy as we do.

FRIENDS & ACQUAINTANCES

We reach a certain point in our lives and all of a sudden we look around and find we are missing some friends. Some have moved on, some have died and some are just different as they aged. You probably know people who have decided at this point in their life, they don't want to go to reunions. Some people don't like to go to reunions such as high school, military, old associations, primarily because when they see these old friends, they see themselves as they really are today.

The problem that I have is that I don't see me as old. I don't think old and I don't really feel old. I guess old is in the eye of the beholder. As some of us will be moving into our new renewalment community, we will be meeting new friends and establishing new relationships. As you answer the following questions, be as honest as you can and then put the new ideas to work for you. It should be a lot of fun.

SOCIAL PLANNING

1. Do you consider yourself a friendly person? **Yes** **No**

2. Do you like people? **Yes** **No**

3. Do you associate with positive people rather than negative people? **Yes** **No**

4. Do you dress well? **Yes** **No**

5. Is your appearance good at this point in your life? **Yes** **No**

6. Are you considerate of others? **Yes** **No**

7. Do you keep your appointments on time? **Yes** **No**

8. Do you have a large circle of friends? **Yes** No

9. Do you respect their opinions? **Yes** No

10. Are you active in your community? **Yes** No

11. Would you like to be more active in the community?
Yes No

12. Are you a good listener? **Yes** No

13. Do you frequently go the "extra mile" to help a friend? **Yes** No

14. Do you encourage others to use their abilities?
Yes No

15. Do you believe that every individual you meet is a potential friend? **Yes** No

16. Can you still remember people's names? **Yes** No

17. Do you entertain enough? Do you want to? **Yes** No

18. Do you have a good sense of humor? **Yes** No

19. Do you try to make a contribution to the lives of others? **Yes** No

20. Do you always make others feel important? **Yes** No

YOUR MENTAL & INTELLECTUAL THINKING

The Secret to Life and the answer to how to Renew in style will be found in the last chapter. You will be amazed at its simplicity and if you have not discovered it yet in your life you will question whether you can still obtain it. The answer is "of course you can."

But then, the real answer may be found in this section of knowing yourself. Take the time to answer these questions as honestly as you can because if you miss, then you will not understand the final chapter. What did Shakespeare say about "know thyself?"

MENTAL ATTITUDES

1. Do you think positively all the time? **Yes No**

2. Do you work at improving your memory? **Yes No**

3. Do you enjoy reading? **Yes No**

4. Do you write letters to friends and loved ones?
Yes No

5. Do you work at verbally communicating with friends?
Yes No

6. Do you try to understand the other side of a discussion? **Yes No**

7. Are you as mentally alert today as you were thirty years ago? **Yes No**

8. Do you have any hobbies? **Yes No**

9. Do you find time to work on your hobbies? **Yes No**

10. Do you spend too much time watching television? **Yes No**

11. Do you look at most problems as an opportunity or challenge? **Yes No**

12. Are you a patient individual? **Yes No**

13. Do you praise more than criticize? **Yes No**

14. Do you take time for cultural and mental developments? **Yes No**

15. Do you subscribe to magazines and other materials that will assist you and give you ideas at this point in your life? **Yes No**

SETTING YOUR GOALS

Now that you have found out what your strengths and weaknesses are, it's time to determine what goals you want to establish. Setting the goal is easy, coming up with a plan to successfully achieve your goal is a little bit harder.

First of all, the best way to start is to sit down at your desk, table or easy chair with a pad, pencil and uninterrupted time. Write out the goal that you want to set. Let me give you an example. Let's say you want to lose twenty pounds. Over what period of time? You always need to have a date or deadline when you start the process. When you set a date it really helps on your physiological clock to work towards the goal. Without a date, it is open ended and very likely you will not achieve your goal.

Think about a football game. At each end of the field it has "goal posts" and there are so many minutes to play. If you watch football you know that the most exciting time of the game is after the two minute warning signal. If the game is close, there are more plays and action in the last two minutes than the rest of the quarter. That is what a time limit does and everyone is running towards their goal. The goal is to win and that is what you are trying to do. Win the Goal! Win the Game!

Goals have to be written. I know, you have been

thinking a lot about your goals and they are in your head and there is no reason to write them down. Wrong! Goals must be written. Let me say that again. Your goals must be in writing. I'm sure you are going to have more than one goal, maybe five, ten, fifty and how can you remember all of them or what you need to do to achieve them.

So, once you have your goal written and set your deadline to achieve it, your next question is, "So how do I develop my plan, what are the solutions?" Before you can come up with "solutions", you need to know what the obstacles are. "If this is what my goal is, what is stopping me from achieving it now?" You know what the obstacles are on just about every goal you will set for yourself.

You start off by making a list of all the reasons you can not achieve the goal. Don't have the money, the education, the time, the desire, the knowledge, someone to help you, whatever is stopping you. You can have two, three or more obstacles why you can't lose the weight, or get a better job, or get that new car and once you know what they are, now all you have to do is come up with the "solutions".

When you look at each obstacle you might come up with four, five or more solutions and when you are all done with your list of obstacles, you could have ten, twenty, fifty or more solutions to achieve the one goal you set for yourself.

The next question you ask yourself is the most important question in this whole equation. Looking over all the solutions and what you must do to achieve that one goal, you ask yourself, "Is it worth it to me?" If the answer is yes, it's a good goal. If you are not willing to do or work on the solutions you have outlined, it's not a good goal, get rid of it or re-evaluate it.

Goal: I want to lose twenty pounds

Date: I want to achieve this goal by (Date)

Obstacles:

1. Don't have time to plan daily menu's

2. Enjoy my ice cream too much.

3. Enjoy my cocktails and tidbits in the evening.

4. No time for exercise.

5. Too many social functions to go to.

6. Enjoy eating out in restaurants.

Solutions:

1. I will sit down with my spouse and enlist their help in planning weekly meals.

2. Will research the right type of foods to eat.

3. Determine what I can give up or eat less of during the week.

4. Do not plan on starving but eat a balanced menu.

5. Give up ice cream and maybe eat it only on Saturdays. Try sugar free ice cream or yogurt as a substitute.

6. Have one glass a wine in the evening and either cut back the snacks in half or altogether.

7. Set a time for exercise.

8. Determine the exercises I will do.

9. Start walking every day.

10. Plan for one dinner a week out in a restaurant.

11. Write out my goals on 3x5 cards and review these during the day to remind me of my goals.

12. Place some pictures of what I used to look like or what I would like to look like in my bathroom, bedroom, etc. to remind me of my goal.

13. Work on developing the discipline to achieve my goals.

Rewards:

10. Look good.

11. Feel good.

12. Lower my blood pressure.

13. Fit into my clothes.

14. Be able to purchase some new, smaller sizes, clothes

15. More energy

Now it is just a matter of keeping track of your results. Remember, it is important to inspect what you expect. You can use this method for setting goals on every other goal you set, no matter the size or value. It works, try it!

CHAPTER 4

LIFE IS GOOD

Life IS good, with its ups and downs. Life is certainly better than the alternative. Some people do exceptionally well throughout their lives while others struggle, lose money, have poor health and suffer other tragedies but that, to tell you the truth, is Life. How you handle Life rather than having Life handle you, is the equation. If we have a plan for our Life, it is a lot better than having no plan or someone else having a plan for us. The important thing is that as we reach what in the past we would have called "retirement", we now look at "renewalment" in a totally new way, and start planning for this whole new era of our lives. It doesn't matter at what age we renew. What matters is that we "think" renewing is a new phase in our life and our aim is to live it to its fullest.

Set your goals. Write out your plan and develop the action that will take you to your goals. When you get up in the morning, no matter how you feel, start your day off positively.

Some thirty plus years ago, I read about Charley "Tremendous" Jones, a successful insurance salesman and renowned speaker. Everything was "tremendous." I thought about that for awhile and decided to come up with a word for me and it was "Fantastic". Well, you can imagine what happened when I started to use it when people would ask me how I was. They laughed, giggled and humphed and wondered who I thought I was. I kept using it until it became a habit. After awhile, I didn't have to think about it; I just automatically said "Fantastic" when anyone asked me how I was. In fact, my first wife Liz would ask me how I was in the morning and if I didn't say "fantastic", she immediately asked me what was wrong.

As I continued to use the word "fantastic" some people began calling me Mr. Fantastic. If I had an appointment to visit an office and they had a marquee outside that welcomed guests, it would say, "Welcome, Mr. Fantastic". This happened on several occasions over the years. At one time in Denver as I went to visit one of the Midas shops for which I was a District Manager, the owner wasn't feeling well. He had to go in for exploratory surgery and asked if I would keep an eye on his shop for a week. Of course I said yes.

His wife came in later that week and she said that they opened him up and then closed him up and gave him six months to live with cancer. She said he wouldn't talk to anyone, not to her, the doctors, or the children. He had been given a death sentence. She asked me to go to the hospital and "make him talk". I didn't know Al that well but I couldn't say no and I certainly didn't know what to say to him. When I got to the hospital, he was walking down the hall with the intravenous drugs on the pole with wheels, and saw me get off the elevator. He stood there looking at me and I didn't say a word. Al spoke first and said, "Fantastic!"

Al lived twelve months before he passed on but I realized the powerful ammunition and truth in the word, Fantastic. It has been a part of me all these years in all my activities and in all that Life has given to me. Some people won't ask me how I am because they know what I'm going to say. Some say "I don't know why I asked, I knew you were going to say that". And sometimes when I leave a message for someone to return my call, I say "my name is Kaufmann, K-A-U-F as in Fantastic M-A-N-N. They laugh; they like it; they comment; and guess what, I love it too. Some people say, "I wish I could say that" and I tell them, "Go ahead and say it" when they reply, "but I don't feel that way," my comment is "Then lie in advance."

The words that you use are the most powerful tools that you have and the words that you say to yourself are the most important. Your brain has a conscious mind and a sub-conscious mind. The sub-conscious mind is like a computer. Every thought, every action you have ever encountered is in there. It is programmed away and the sub-conscious mind does not think for it self. You are the programmer and it responds to what you put in. So if you put in negative thoughts, it responds accordingly. If you put in positive thoughts, it responds in kind. So why not start the day off with a positive, exciting word, whether you mean it, or feel it, or not? Use any word that has a positive meaning for you like tremendous, wonderful, awesome, super, great and, if you want, Fantastic.

When my wife Judy and I wake up in the morning the first thing I ask her is "How are you this morning?" She immediately and always says, "Fantastic". That starts our day. The tone is set and it ends up that way when we go to bed. In between, we pray, discuss business positively and talk about good things at the end of the day as we have our glass of wine after work, listening to soft music.

Life is good. It all depends on how you look at it and the words you use to describe it. Is your glass half full or is it half empty? The choice is yours to make.

CHAPTER 5

LIFE LEADING UP TO RENEWALMENT

Life is what we live each and every day. It would be wonderful if we could all say Life is great and we have no problems. But we know that is not realistic. Life has its many problems and characteristics that each one of us has to live through. How we handle those problems determines how we get through life, how much we enjoy life, and how we can continue to live each and every day in a robust manner that makes life worth living.

Many of us are faced with problems beyond our control, yet when we are confronted by those problems, how we control ourselves, our thinking, and our attitudes, determines how we can get past the problem. When obstacles are thrown at us during our life time, we need to discover the ways to get over, around or through the problem and continue on with our life.

Death has a way of messing up your life. Liz, my first wife of thirty three years, became ill at age 51. From the time she was diagnosed, she passed away within two months. No one is ever prepared for something like this and even though I knew she was terminal, nothing would allow me to think in those terms. I read everything I could on her condition. I researched and talked to everyone I could and hoped and prayed that everything was fine. And when it wasn't, I went through the many modes that many people in this situation do face, from anger to grief to just not understanding why this happened.

After Liz passed away, I was invited to a grief session with about ten or twelve other people who had lost a loved one. As I listened that night to them telling their stories and listening to their grief, it burdened me so that I couldn't take theirs and mine also, and I did not go back.

A friend we had known through our daughters and who had lost her husband earlier, invited me to a widowed group. As I sat there listening to their stories and hearing them live in the past, where some of their spouses had died years before, I realized that I would not be going back to that group either.

This same friend then invited me to a singles group. As I sat there listening to the conversation, she looked over at me and said, "You won't be coming back, will you?"

She was right, I didn't go back. I went forward. Liz had passed away in August and when December came around, I had no desire to spend that time with any of my four children and their families. I was still in grief mode. I made plans to go to California, from my home in El Paso. The plan was to visit my 100 year old uncle in

San Diego on Christmas Eve, then drive up to San Juan Capistrano on Christmas day to visit my Father and Step-mother. From there, after a couple of days of playing golf, I would head over to Las Vegas and spend New Years with an old friend who was recently divorced.

As I was sitting having Christmas dinner with my father and step-mother, the thought entered my mind that I was going to end my trip tomorrow and head back to El Paso. I told my dad and he was disappointed since he had scheduled golf with some friends. I called my friend in Las Vegas, said, "Sorry", and headed back.

As I left San Juan Capistrano, I had a note pad sitting next to me and over the next eight hours, I stopped for gas but had no coffee or anything to eat. I wrote as I drove. I started setting goals for the rest of my life. I was going back to flying airplanes, which I loved. I was going to take dance lessons. I was going to join the YMCA for exercise and get my health and weight where it should be. I set many other goals and had a complete plan laid out by the time I got back.

New Year's Eve I was invited out with my friends Judy and Mike Wendt to a dinner and show at a local nite club. That was the evening I met Margie Reeder. Three months later we were married and that marriage lasted thirteen years until Margie died in June, 2004.

After we were married, I realized what was missing from

the lives of the people in the grief seminars, the widows and widowers group and the singles group. In fact, I went back and gave the widowed group a talk on what they should be looking for. I discovered that they had been living in the past, constantly thinking of the deceased, and in some cases divorced spouse and not giving any thought to the future. They had no goals, no plans, nothing to take them toward a higher plane in their life. They had gotten to the bridge but they were stymied. What they had to do was "get over the bridge." What you have to do is get over it and get on with it and live life to its fullest.

In March of 2004, Margie started complaining about stomach pains but she just shrugged it off as food poisoning. When the pains continued, she went to a doctor. It was almost a month before it was diagnosed as colon cancer. An immediate operation was arranged but the cancer had gotten too far and the doctor told me it was terminal.

At the point in the hospital when we arranged for her to have Hospice care, I sat with her and began thinking about my next life and started to write down the goals that I would be dealing with for the future. Having been in this place once before and being with my first wife as her life slowly passed away and knowing what lay ahead, I knew what I had to do this time. It is not easy, but understanding grief as I had, I knew the best way to get through it was to think of the future and what life lay ahead, especially at the age of 70.

After her Celebration of Life Service, I went back to work and re-arranged my priorities and started working toward the new goals. Life comes at you hard but it is how you accept it, plan for it and develop the proper attitudes that get you through the difficult parts. I am now 73 and my goals, dreams and aspirations are written down in a large three ring notebook. These give me direction as I live life with my beautiful third wife, Judy, and we plan every day for the future.

Renewalment comes fast, but you know what, with goals and a plan of action, you can live to the fullest every day of your life. Just ask Judy and me how we enjoy each day with EELM.

CHAPTER 6

MANAGE YOUR LIFE AS YOU WOULD YOUR BUSINESS

Over the years I gave talks around the country and worked with many companies on success, goals, management ideas, and marketing plans. It is interesting how many of them had no plans at all. Goals were thought of but not written down. They were elusive or non- existent. Some were working from the seat of their pants and of course, some knew exactly where they were going and how to get there.

Statistics will tell you that only 3% of the population has a written, specific goal and a plan on how to get there. This applies to businesses as well. If a company is going to borrow money from a lending institution, the first thing the bank wants to know is, "What's your plan?"

A year and a half ago, we applied for a franchise with a leading International real estate company and had to fill out all the paper work, financial statements and goals and objectives that we hoped to accomplish with this company. I diligently provided all the information and put it in a format as recommended by their representative. Just prior to sending it in, I wasn't happy with the way it looked, so added some pizzazz to the package, with our specific goals and how we do our job now and how we planned on doing it better in the future.

I wasn't totally satisfied with the package, but time was of the essence, so it was overnighted that day. Our representative told us that a committee would review the package and that they were selective on who they chose. Sometimes even large companies would get turned down, and we were a "start up" with them, so we were told not to expect too much. To our surprise and joy we were quickly selected that day and comments were made as to the professionalism and how good our package was. In fact, we were told that our package was sent to other staffers to show them how it should be done.

I was surprised because I wasn't all that impressed with what I had sent in, but I knew it had good information and told a story. It amazed me that other larger companies were turned down because of not having their goals and plans written down. My thoughts were, "How have they been doing business all this time without some specific plan to guide them?" This really brought home the idea of how important everything we do in our company to establish goals and plans and on how to get where we want to go is so urgently needed.

We have been with this major franchise company for a year and a half now and just the other day I received a call from our business consultant who stated that we have had a 410% increase in business since last year.

Our company has goals and all our associates must have goals. If my goal is to achieve a certain amount of sales in a year and I don't know what our associate's goals are and what they are striving for, there is no way we can achieve the company goal. They go hand in hand. If the associate's total goals don't equal the company goal, we have a problem. If their goals exceed our goals, then victory is in sight. In November of each year, I have a meeting with each associate and go over goal setting in general, discuss the company goals, discuss their goals, and bring them all together for the combined success of everyone.

I truly feel that the best thing that I can do for my associates is to help them become totally goal directed and to understand all that it has to offer. They can achieve whatever success they want in life by having goals and a plan to get there. If you can help enough people get what they want, you can get what you want. It's that easy.

CHAPTER 7

OH MY ACHING BACK

When we reach the Renewalment age, and that can be anywhere from the fifties on up, and we look forward to a happy and successful life, one of the more important things to consider is your health. What good is it to Renew and not be able to enjoy it?

You remember the old saying, "If I knew I was going to live this long I would have taken better care of myself". One of the first things you need to do is take stock of your overall health at this very moment. Do you have any physical problems? If so, can they be taken care of or made better? If not, how can you manage these in Renewalment?

Once you have reviewed your Physical questions and discovered what areas you need to set goals on and what areas you want to make better, just make your list and get started.

Sounds easy doesn't it? But at this point in time as you think back to when you where young and just getting started in life, we didn't have time to exercise or work out. We enjoyed eating and drinking and worked hard. We promised ourselves that in time we would take care of ourselves and lose some weight. We'd get to the doctor one of these days but we are too busy right now. Those that smoked probably knew better and one of these days they would quit but it sure eases the tension now. And of course, if you quit smoking your weight would go up and you didn't have time to exercise, so we'll worry about that later.

Guess what? Later is here. Time goes by fast and Life Happens and then its time for Renewalment and you know what, I just don't feel as good as I would like to. I'm a few pounds overweight and I've got this cough from smoking and a few aches and pains here and there and if I just felt a little better, I could enjoy my Renewalment a lot more.

Well, you can feel as good as you desire to feel. Take some action to solve some of the problems that you have developed over the years. The first step is to go over the questions on Physical planning, find out where you need to have some action, write those goals down and then develop the action steps necessary to start feeling better.

Are you in good health at the present time? Is good health important to you? It will be vitally important if you intend to maintain that good health as you change your lifestyle. If you have some problems, determine what they are and what can be done to either correct them or improve on them.

An easy thing to consider as we age, but not necessarily

a simple one, is exercise. Exercise can be as simple as walking a little every day. Also get our weight to where we want it by being careful what we put in our mouths. Decide to quit smoking if that is the case and then Do It. Answer the questions, set your goals, write out your action steps and then Do It.

W. Clement Stone, a successful Insurance Executive, wealthy author of success books, and great speaker, stated that one of the most important things he ever did was to "Do It Now!" He wrote that down everywhere he could see it and then just Did It. That is what you have to do with your Physical planning. Decide to Do It and Do It!

I like the old cliché, "If you continue to do what you've always done, you will continue to get what you've always gotten". Renewalment is changing your ways and now you have to change your habits if you are going to live long enough to enjoy it.

Judy and I have an exercise room downstairs in our home. It has an incline sit up board, a stationary bike, a Total Gym that Chuck Norris promotes, plus weights. We do sit-ups, lift weights, make good use of the Total Gym, and ride the bike five miles every other day. At 74 and 65 we do quite well with our equipment and we do have to make that extra effort in the morning, but we Do It. We know that walking has to become a part of the regimen and have added that to the other three days.

We work hard at eating the right foods but we don't feel miserable. Judy is a gourmet cook and spends a lot of her time reviewing recipes to try for their taste and health benefits. We keep those we like and forget about the others. It is fun, interesting and beneficial and then we can share it with our friends.

We enjoy a glass of wine in the evening or a cocktail but never in excess. A glass of wine can be healthful for you and one is all we need. We look forward to many good years together and our health is important to us. So many people end up in their retirement years taking care of one another and never get to enjoy the time they saved up to be together and do the things they always wanted to do.

Make your Health one of your top priorities as you enter into Renewalment so that you can enjoy it for all its wonderfulness.

CHAPTER 8

EELM

E E L M. Doesn't sound like anything special but this is probably the most important part of Judy's and my relationship since we met and married.

When Judy telephoned her long time friend, Nancy, to tell her we were planning to marry, Nancy ended the conversation with "enjoy every luscious moment." As Judy and I discussed this later, we thought it was so profound that we had to do something with it, so we formed the EELM Club. We decided to come up with some rules for the club and began listing the headings for the ten basic rules. It took us about a month to come up with ideas, discuss them, change or add to them and finally agree on what was important to us. Following are the rules and bylaws as we developed them.

ENJOY EVERY LUSCIOUS MOMENT
RULES & BYLAWS

1. Membership in this organization shall be solely and lovingly co-joined by Judy and Lou from this day forward and through eternity.

2. The Goal of EELM members is to achieve and maintain unconditional Love.

3. Love and mutual respect shall be shown to each other and shall abound.

4. Love shall rule everything, including all meetings, get togethers and being together by ourselves.

5. Other people may be encouraged to form their own EELM Club if the current two members consider them worthy of these ideas.

6. A sense of humor is vital to this relationship but never at the expense of one another.

7. Truthfulness, Honesty and Trust are the foundation of the EELM Club.

8. There will be no secrets between each other except pleasant surprises and gifts.

9. To live each day one day at a time with each other and live that day to its fullest.

10. We place this union and our lives in God's hands and will let Him Guide and direct us in our life, now and forever more.

The EELM Club has guided us since its inception and

in the three years that we have been married, we have never had a fight or serious disagreement. We attribute that to our rules. We do follow Rule #9 very closely because it is so important. "To live each day one day at a time with each other and live that day to its fullest."

From the time we wake up in the morning, our attitudes are positive. Still in bed, I ask my wife how she is and she always says, "Fantastic." That starts the day, each and every day. We have our coffee, read the paper, discuss our activities for the day and get started. The time we spend together is positive and reinforcing. We eliminate negatives as best we can. It is kind of like the time during World War II when one of the rallying songs was "eliminate the negative, accentuate the positive and don't mess with Mr. In-between."

To some this may sound Pollyanna, but to us, it is a beautiful way to spend the day and our time together. We take everything one day at a time. Our goals for tomorrow are set and what happened yesterday is past. We are working on today,

Living each day to it's fullest. What is the fullest? At this stage in your life when you have Renewed, what is important? Exercise is something we do every other day and we try to stay with the program. If for any reason we miss a day we just get back on schedule as quickly as we can. If part of the body is aching, we work those parts that don't ache and figure out solutions to cure the aches on the other parts.

If weight is a problem, and when isn't it, then we just have to take it one day at a time. Watch what we eat and what we put into our bodies. It does take discipline and heaven knows how difficult that can be sometimes but we do it one day at a time.

A new program that we have added to our lives is what we call Gourmet Saturday. This is the day that we come up with a gourmet menu, something different, could be unique, that perhaps we haven't had before. It will take extra preparation but we do it together in the kitchen. This is the one day that we may go off our diet or cut loose a little but we are just living that one day to its fullest. Gourmet Saturday! What a treat.

Living each day to it's fullest. Isn't that what life is all about? To be enjoyed, to have fun, to build memories, regardless of your age. To be renewed as you get older and not be thinking of the negatives or the worse things that can happen.

To live each day, one day at a time, with each other and live that day to it's fullest.

Rule number 10 says it all. "We place this union and our lives in God's hands and will let him guide and direct us in our life, now and forever more."

As we each look at our past lives and how we lived those years, we know that God brought us together. Our meeting was brought about because of Edith Baker, a wonderful family friend of Judy's parents. We thank God for Edith.

A best seller of a few years ago, A Purpose Driven Life, stated that God has a plan for each and every life, even before you are born. Having read that book together in the first months of our marriage, we have come to believe how true that is. We look at our lives today and how we complement each other in everything we do, from the home care with Judy's parents to the real estate company, to our daily lives. We pray together daily and we let Him direct us in our daily lives. We pray for guidance, help, direction and the ability to help others and we listen for the answers. We listen and look around us daily and never worry about things because we have put our lives in God's hands.

You need to do the same. It doesn't matter where you are in your life today as it relates to God, you just need to talk with him and ask for his help. It is simple. It is easy. It is as simple and easy as saying, "Hi God, I've got a problem." Or a question or a statement, but just begin talking. As the Bible says, you can go in the "closet" but you can do it anywhere. In your bed, the shower, your car, the park, wherever you decide to do it, but Do It!

"We place this union and our lives in God's hands and will let him guide and direct us in our life, now and forever more."

If you would like to join the E E L M Club, just send us your names, address, e-mail, and we will send you a copy of the Rules and By-Laws, ready to display where you can see it every day.

CHAPTER 9

WHERE IS YOUR POPLAR FOREST?

Thomas Jefferson's Poplar Forest is in Virginia, about 90 miles from Monticello, his home. It was his retreat. A place to go to get away from everything, yet he didn't begin working on his Poplar Forest until he was 63. He was still working on it at age 80. It is very possible that Renewing or Renewalment was begun by Thomas Jefferson. After all, he founded the University of Virginia when he was 76 years old.

So, where is your Poplar Forest? Do you have one? Have you thought about one? Do you care? When we renew, some of us renew in style and have enough money to do whatever we want. Some are debt free but not enough cash to do a lot of things or travel much. Many retire with little or just enough to get by on and certainly some retire with almost nothing.

Social Security by itself from one spouse certainly may not be enough and with two can maintain them. If the couple is lucky enough to have other retirement programs or military service to add to it, they are ok.

In the forties, fifties and sixties, folks would get a job with a company and work thirty or so years and then retire with a nice monthly pension. That is not happening today. Companies are using their pension money to stay in business and some are being raided by takeover companies. Airline pilots who had good retirement programs and worked all those years are now finding out if the company goes bankrupt, they are losing their pensions. This is happening with many companies. Enron is one which is well known that left everyone who worked there without anything.

So here you are ready to Renew. It may be what you planned and then again, it may not be. Too late to do anything about it now or even make the money to replace what you may have lost. A headline in the paper recently stated, "Retirement not all it's cracked up to be." That certainly may be the case, but we are not retiring, we are Renewing. We are not going into "seclusion."

As the definition of Renew states, it means "to begin or take up again, to restore or replenish, to revive, re-establish, make new as if new again. To be restored to a former state." Well, if your income is not where you want it to be when you Renew, then you need to start taking stock of where you are and where you would like to go.

We had thought we would like to have our Poplar Forest somewhere away from our home in Bella Vista, near a lake or resort area, to get away on weekends. Then we realized we already live in a resort with eight lakes and eight golf courses. People come here to enjoy weekends, so by golly, so should we. Instead of buying the second home somewhere, we purchased the empty lot next to us which we now call "the ranch." We have plans for the ranch that should keep us busy for as long as we care to be. We plan on building a Garden Railroad with a Railroad Station Gazebo and will be a great place to relax and enjoy our hobbies. It is not exactly the Poplar Forest, but it is our Poplar Forest. Thomas Jefferson worked on his retreat from age 63 to age 80, so this should keep us busy in our renewalment.

If money is a problem at this point in your life, there are many ways you can make extra dollars if you so desire. You may want to stay busy and still meet other people. Wal Mart loves to hire retired folks to be greeters at their stores. What type of work did you do in your career? Is there a service that you can offer the public today based on your past experience? Write a book, offer a service on the Internet, set up your own website, sell a product over your website, sell a service on your site, share your experiences for a fee. Be creative. Mastermind with some of your friends and if you are not sure what this is, we'll cover it in another chapter.

So what happens if you don't have your Poplar Forest? Does it really matter? Not really. What matters is that we learn from the likes of Thomas Jefferson, over two hundred years ago. Maybe we can't write a Declaration of Independence or start a University but we can read like he did. We can think, plan and create like he did. We can keep going like he did just like the energizer bunny. Just keep on keeping on. Jefferson "retired" as President of the United States at age 66 and then Renewed his life for another seventeen years. Why not follow his example and start planning your "Poplar Forest" right now.

CHAPTER 10

MASTERMINDING IN RENEWALMENT

One of the keys to a successful and happy renewalment is to associate yourself with other positive people. Remember, "Eliminate the negative." I will not associate with negative people nor will I have them working with me in our company. If I cannot get them to change their thinking from negative to positive, then I will ask them to leave our organization.

In his book, Think and Grow Rich, Napoleon Hill talks about Masterminding with other like people. The secret is to find two, three, four or five other folks that have Renewed or are getting ready to Renew and who want to share goals, ideas, positive thoughts and plans. Then get together once a week for coffee, breakfast or lunch, and share. Each meeting one of the members has a topic or goal he would like to share. Maybe he/she needs help in planning the goal or what action steps are necessary. Napoleon Hill states that there are two characteristics of the Master Mind Principle. One is economic in nature and the other is psychic. "No two minds ever come together without thereby creating a third, invisible, intangible force which may be likened to a third mind."

Over the years I have been involved in a couple of Master Mind Groups and one thing it has done was develop life long friendships. I have seen people go from one career to another and be successful. I have seen people change direction in their lives based on the friendships and discussions at Master Mind Groups. What better way when we have reached Renewalment age than to find others of similar situations and get together to share stories, ideas, goals and plans for the future. All it takes is a "like mind."

There is a coffee shop next to our office. When we go over there are always groups of men of renewalment age talking about their golf game, their aches and pains or the news of the day. Let's face it; the news of the day has to be the most negative of all. I remember years ago a friend stating that he only read the sports page because he would rather read about men's accomplishments than their failures. A Master Mind Group sitting there discussing the positive aspects of life and plans for the future would be felt by all who would go by. The power and the force that can be transmitted from a Master Mind Group in the right direction can be awesome. Andrew Carnegie, Henry Ford and Thomas Edison all participated in Master Mind Groups and great fortunes were made as were great friendships.

Who's to say that a group of people Renewed couldn't get together and discuss issues that could have lasting effects for all? Get a copy of Think and Grow Rich and follow the outline that is discussed. Find the people that fit in with your thinking, who have positive thoughts or would like to have more positive thoughts and get started. Start with one and grow from there. Find one like thinking person and begin. Whatever your situation in life is, if you wanted to change, amend, redirect or add to it, this is the way to go. As Zig Ziglar says, who at this writing is eighty years old and still putting on dynamic seminars, "Get rid of your stinking thinking."

Paul J. Meyer, who founded Success Motivation Institute and has been selling Success for over forty years in many countries throughout the world, in the billions of dollars, is now eighty years old and still going strong. You know what this says to me?

Be positive, goal directed, have a plan and live a long life. Remember, "Success is the progressive realization of worthwhile predetermined personal goals."

Associate with positive friends, read positive books. The greatest power we have is the Power to Choose. It would be difficult to control others or what they do or say, but we have control over ourselves. I choose to be positive and I choose to be Fantastic. What do you choose? Make Renewalment the best time of your life. Enjoy life to its fullest and above all, E E L M.

CHAPTER 11

THE PROBLEMS SENIORS FACE TODAY

It is 2008 and life is changing as we knew it back in the fifties, sixties, etc. When we look at what can be considered the most pressing problems we face today, I would say "gas prices", Gas is selling over $3.50 a gallon and the possibility of it coming down and getting back to where it was just a year ago, I don't believe will happen.

The reasons for the high prices are many, but specifically, the world is running out of oil. It took over one hundred fifty million years to make the oil and in just over one hundred years we have already used over half of all the oil reserves. When the oil is gone, there is no more. Certainly there will have to be other forms of energy sources and I'm sure scientific discoveries will be made, but in the meantime, today, what do we do?

Oil is responsible for so many of our products and activities today and when that oil is depleted, what is going to happen? Third world nations are expanding and as a result they are making a bigger demand for what oil is available. Then there are those nations that produce oil and are having major conflicts within their country, so that production is down. There are those countries that do not like the United States and so reduce their exports to us. Tie in the political unrest throughout the world, especially in the Arab world where the major oil reserves are and where the price of a barrel of oil is established.

The United States understands the situation and in looking for alternative energy sources, develops Ethanol as a new energy solution, which takes corn to make. All of a sudden, food prices have gone up. It costs more for the eighteen wheelers to transport the food and other products because of the high price of oil, and less corn is available to be used for food.

The price of everything we use daily is going up. Airplane tickets go up and travel drops off. Vacations are cut. Larger cars and SUV's don't sell, and on and on. And here we are, renewed, on a fixed income, and trying to figure just how to survive in this whole new ball game.

I haven't painted a pretty picture but this is what is happening and we have to deal with it. So, the question is, how do we plan for our life in renewalment, considering all these issues? What can we do about these situations? Well, as far as all the price increases, nothing. We have no control over any of these matters. The only control we have is over ourselves and that is the issue with which we have to deal.

First of all, how do we "think" regarding all of these things that are currently happening? If we dwell on them and get upset over them, then we have lost. We need to say to ourselves, "Gas prices, wow! It's going to cost me x number of dollars more every time I fill up and that's the price I have to pay." You really need to sit down and work on your plan of action that deals with your financial well being.

How much more is gas going to cost you monthly than what you had been paying? Are you willing to pay that increase? Can you rework your budget where you cut back on something else? I think there are a lot of questions you need to research. Based on what I was paying last year at this time for gas and that it could be costing us four dollars a gallon shortly, that comes out to an increase of twenty three dollars every fill up. I usually fill my car once a week so that is about one hundred dollars more a month. Judy fills up about twice a month and her numbers will be close to mine, so we figure that the increases are going to cost us about one hundred and fifty dollars more a month. Do I have the right car that I need to be driving at this time in my life? Do we need two cars? These are the types of questions you need to look at also.

If my monthly expenses are increasing, is there any way I can increase my income? Would it benefit me to do some part time work to offset the increase? Is that important to me? If we like to travel by car, am I driving the right car for my trips? Can I plan my life where I live right now to reduce my driving and still enjoy all the things I like to do? Do I plan my week to shop for all my needs at one time to reduce my travels?

Some of you might remember back in the early fifties, like I do, when I worked at a service station, and when gas sold for twenty cents a gallon.

In 1957 I purchased my first new car right off the showroom floor. It was a Fairlane Ford 500 for which I paid $3,000. In 2004 I purchased a pre-owned Lincoln Town car for $22,000. That $22,000 was more than my first house we bought in River Plaza, New Jersey in 1957. Times have changed over the years, as have the cost of things versus the income we make. As they say, "It's all relative."

So, how do we cope with the changes today in our world? As we have said, the two things which are sure about life are that times change and stuff happens. Globalization is happening and the American way of life is changing and how we adapt our attitudes and our positioning for the future will determine how well we can live in Renewalment.

I have worked hard all my life for those things that I can afford and I enjoy my Lincoln Town car. It is safe and comfortable but only gets about twenty miles a gallon. There are those folks out there who would expect you to drive a hybrid or something less of a car. Presently, we have two vehicles. Since my wife is a caregiver for her parents and we still spend time at the office, it is essential to have the cars. Maybe at some point we will get down to one, but if you can put it in your budget along with the increase in gas prices and still maintain your lifestyle, then go for it. It is your Renewalment and after having worked hard all your adult life, you owe it to yourself to Live Life to its Fullest, One Day at a Time.

CHAPTER 12

RENEWING WHEN WE STILL HAVE PARENTS

When Judy and I met three years ago, she was living with her parents as she was taking care of them. She had lived in France for several years and returned because her mother was aging and was diagnosed with the first stages of Alzheimer's. Judy had always said that her mother had always "been there" for her and that she would "be there" for her mother.

When Judy and I married, I also took on the responsibility of caring for her mother and step-father, knowing how important this was to her. For the first six months we lived across the street from her folks. Each morning Judy went over to fix breakfast before going to work. During the week Meals on Wheels delivered lunch and at night, we fixed dinner and had the folks over to our house to eat and play dominoes, seven days a week.

As the disease progressed and the efforts became greater, we realized that we had to find some type of program that would give us more flexibility but still give them the care that they deserved. Was it time to put them in some sort of Assisted Living or in a home where they could get constant supervision? How would we pay for it? Lots of questions and so we started to do some research. Judy looked at the various help programs that were available and what kind of assistance was available to help with the medications. Prescription drugs to help the folks were expensive and taking almost all of their monthly income, which was not a lot.

We talked with our pastor, organizations and companies that assist the elderly and received lots of reading material. We read, researched and discussed. One idea we saw was obtaining a Reverse Mortgage on their home to assist with home health care. This really seemed to be one of the best options because they could stay right in their own home and their own surroundings and still get the treatment and care they deserved with family being close.

Here we are in our sixties and seventies, newly weds, looking forward to travel, taking time to enjoy ourselves and we have "kids" to take care of. That's what we call the folks, the kids, and we have fun with that. We try not to make it a chore because we really do love them and want to provide them quality of life.

As we studied the Reverse Mortgage idea, it seemed to be the best way to go. Their home did not have a mortgage, so they had all that equity. The Reverse Mortgage is based on the idea that the mortgage company will loan them up to 80% of the appraised value of the home today. Reverse Mortgages are covered by the Federal Government and through the Department of HUD, which makes sure everything is done correctly.

The loan is established just the same as if you were applying for a new one, but instead, when it is approved, you have access to the money. You can take it in a lump sum, or take it as a line of credit and get the money as you need it, or you can take it monthly with an automatic deposit in your account.

The loan is made to the folks who own the house and they have to be over the age of 50 to qualify. In our case, being they were in the nineties, Judy had power of attorney and so she applied for it and signed all the paper work. The mortgage companies and banks want to make sure that it is a legitimate loan and that someone isn't taking advantage of an elderly person or couple.

After a mistake or two, we took the loan on a monthly basis and it is an automatic deposit into the folk's bank account, for which Judy has power of attorney. There are no payments to be made during the life of the loan and the folks can stay and live in the house as long as they desire or are able. Only when they have moved or gone does the loan need to be paid off. At that time, you get the house ready to sell and put it on the market and sell it. Whatever proceeds are left after the loan is paid off will go into the estate.

The next step was to find a Caregiver. We contacted

various organizations who provide them but the cost was greater than we felt we could afford. We decided to write a job description of what we wanted done for the folks and placed a classified ad in the local newspaper. We received many calls, set up a few interviews and found the person we were looking for. She had experience, and good references, lived fairly close and had a mature but pleasant personality. The caregiver works five days a week and Judy takes over on Fridays and Sundays. She sees to it that her Mom gets up and gets dressed, eats, takes her medicines and in the evening we bring them to our home, now four miles away, for a nice dinner and a game of dominoes. We take them home before nine, give them their medicines and they can still take care of themselves to get to bed ok at night.

We have enough capital planned for five years. With three more to go we are doing everything we can to give the folks the quality of life that they deserve and you can do the same. We cared for our kids when we are young, and we care for the "kids" when we renew, but if you plan it all out and take care of all the details, it will work out smoothly and be better than you anticipated. Although they forget a lot (even your name sometimes), the smile and quick wit are still there and make it all that much more worthwhile.

CHAPTER 13

FUN AND GAMES IN RENEWALMENT

"Happiness is a voyage, not a destination, there is no better time to be happy than.....NOW!"

As I neared Renewalment, many of my friends who had "retired" would tell me that they didn't know how they got everything done before because they are so busy now. Those friends that seemed to be the happiest were the ones who were the busiest. The biggest gripe seemed to be "there is not enough time to get everything done."

One of my goals most of my life was to learn to play the piano. I had started when I was a youngster but somehow along the way, my aunt wanted her piano back and there went my lessons. Sixty years later I mentioned to my new wife one of my life's goals and she surprised me on our first Christmas with an electronic keyboard with all the bells and whistles. When I said I needed a teacher, she found one and I began taking piano lessons after all those years. I am taking a hiatus from lessons right now but I can play the piano-- even a little Beethoven. All it takes to do it well is practice and I plan to do lots of it during my Renewal years. If I can do it, anyone can. Trust me.

Fifteen years ago when I lived in Las Cruces, New Mexico and was selling real estate, a friend asked if I would like to write a weekly real estate article for the Las Cruces Sun News. I jumped at the opportunity and wrote one each week for a year until we moved. It was fun, interesting, informative and a way for me to gain knowledge in my business field. I decided I wanted to write some books and set the goal. When this is completed it will be the first one but I also have another one half completed and a third with an outline started. It is just a matter of deciding to do it and then do it! Do you have that dream or desire? Get started. Do it now!

How many days in a week in Renewalment?
6 Saturdays and 1 Sunday

Travel is one of the goals we have set for Renewalment but these days with high gas prices, some adjustments may have to be made. Planning ahead is the best thing you can do for those trips you want to make but certainly, spontaneity is good too. When you set your goals earlier in the book, just where have you planned to go? Did you know that most people spend more time planning their vacations then they do in planning their lives?

A local Bank recently published some information about a travel website that helps you plan where to stay, eat and play around the world. It contains information from databases previously available only to travel agents for a fee.

www.ProfessionalTravelGuide.com does not book travel. You plan at the site, then book through any travel agent or booking site. Lots of good information to help with your future travel needs.

What is the common term for someone who enjoys work and refuses to renew? Nuts!

Do you have any hobbies? When asked that question before, I used to say "putzing", which in my mind took in a lot of things without being specific. Nowadays, Judy and I are into specifics. Judy likes to work on her photographs, pictures that she took all over Europe while she lived there. She can convert negatives to the computer and print the pictures from there to place in albums.

When I first met my wife I belonged to a Model Railroad Club here in Bella Vista. I had always loved model trains and have a pretty good collection of HO and O27. I took Judy to one of our member's home for a social and to look at his Garden Railroad in the back yard. Judy fell in love with the idea. Soon we purchased our first G Scale train and ran it around the Christmas tree during the holidays.

As we got closer to Renewalment, we talked about the Garden Railroad we wanted to build. However our lot with its steep incline didn't provide the best layout possibilities so we purchased the lot next to us for that purpose. Design plans are underway with a train station style Gazebo as the primary feature with the trains around it.

Hobbies can be simple or complex. They can get started and never be finished, a work always in progress that gives you something to do that you enjoy. What are your hobbies and what kind of fun is in store for you?

When you are in Renewalment, what do you do all week? Monday to Friday, nothing: Saturday and Sunday I rest.

To compute or not to compute, that is the question. If you are like me, I came along before the computer generation. I was in to my fifties when I really got to look at the computer and it was beyond me. If I had problems with the computer or cd's or DVD players, I had to call my grandson.

Early on I took a computer college course at the Las Cruces Community College. Slowly but surely I began to work with the computer but just when you thought you knew something about it, they came out with the newest version. During my business years it has always been important to have a secretary or assistant or in my case, a wife, who understands computer, to be there when you need help, which is often.

If you don't have a computer at home, buy one. For the capability to write letters, write books, keep your finances current, and work with the internet, plus e-mailing has become the communication of choice for your kids, grandkids and old friends. It is a way to stay in touch with what is happening in the world today. If you have any question or need to know anything about your health or well being, just go on the internet. Everything you ever wanted to know is right there on Google.

You are probably saying, "I'm too old to learn computers now" but you're not. You can find someone to hook it up and give you a few lessons. There are all kinds of books out there. If you can read you can learn. My advice to you is, if you don't have a computer, get one and if you want to be a step ahead in many ways, get yourself a Lap Top.

At church today I was talking with the gentleman sitting behind us. I mentioned the book I was writing and he said that he always wanted to write a book because he really has a story to tell. I'm telling you what I told him, "JUST DO IT!"

CHAPTER 14

"IT SEEMS JUST YESTERDAY THAT I WAS YOUNG"

I received an e-mail early on this year and this is what it said:

"You know, time has a way of moving quickly and catching you unaware of the passing years.

It seems just yesterday that I was young, just married and embarking on my new life with my mate. And yet in a way, it seems like eons ago, and I wonder where all the years went. I know that I lived them all...."

Life is to be lived and as the song says, "I didn't promise you a rose garden." As I write these last chapters I look at it as a beginning and do not worry about where the years went. I look at the pictures on my wall and notice me with Ronald Reagan in California when he was running for Governor. I see me shaking hands with LBJ in the White House and remember it oh so clearly. A picture and letter from Dick Nixon and then me in a sailor suit and an Air Force uniform and those wonderful memories.

And then I think, this isn't the end, it is just the beginning. Just like that old truism that says, "Today is the first day of the rest of your life." I also like the one that says "Yesterday is a canceled check, tomorrow is a promissory note, today is ready cash, so spend it wisely."

How do you think? Is that glass half empty or half full? In the Bible, Luke says, "and Jesus said, all things are possible to him that believes." He did not say some things or a few things, he said All things are possible if you believe. What do you believe?

Another verse in the Bible that I always thought was written for sales people is Matthew, Chapter 7, verse 7. "Ask, and it shall be given you; seek, and ye shall find; knock, and it shall be opened unto you: For every one that asketh receiveth; and he that seeketh findeth; and to him that knocketh it shall be opened."

This really says it all about Renewalment. Ask, Seek and Knock. Ask the right questions. Ask for help; ask for direction at this time in your life. Seek answers, new associates, and positive people to associate with. Knock on doors. Knock on my door to talk about Renewalment and then when you don't think you know for sure yet, knock on your head and say, "Just what are my goals for the rest of my life?"

The answers to Life's questions abound. They are all around us and Retirement may be the end but Renewalment is just the beginning. Some of the best advice

I ever found, I read somewhere and it went something like this. "I have read every book on success I could find, Think and Grow Rich, Success through a Positive Mental Attitude, How to Make Friends and Influence People. I have listened and watched all the positive tapes and videos with Tom Hopkins, Earl Nightingale and many more and have attended many Success Seminars with Zig Ziglar, Norman Vincent Peale and Paul Harvey and more, and it all boils down to this.....

DECIDE TO DO IT...........AND THEN DO IT!"

RENEW YOUR LIFE FOR THE REST OF YOUR LIFE

As we take this new concept of life and put it to work in our lives, what really is new and different from the past? The only thing different is the words. We are changing Retire to Renew and Retirement to Renewalment. We are taking words that according to Webster's Dictionary are negative and replacing them with positive words and direction.

We have talked about Goals and that is nothing new. We have talked about different Attitudes and that is nothing new. We have talked about your Thinking, and now, that could be new if you changed it. Change the way you think about retirement. Change the fact that you are not coming into the end of your life but the beginning. What does age have to do with anything? I think I play golf better today then when I was in my thirties.

I can honestly tell you that sex is better in my seventies than it was in my thirties. I think I'm a lot smarter today with more experience. What happened yesterday doesn't count anymore. You have to think out of the box; you need to be creative; you have to get rid of stinking thinking.

There are many things that I would share with all of you and a few of the ideas are these. If you are in a relationship and love is there, don't let it die. Take each area of your life, set your goals, and write them all out. It has to be written. It has to be written. I cannot say that more clearly, your goals have to be written. Each day, make your To Do List. What is it you want to get accomplished. Write it down, set your priorities. I love to make To Do lists. It is fun to cross out those items that are accomplished. It is a great joy to achieve goals, small, medium or large. That is what Success is all about.

You need to have something to look forward to in your life each day. "History has demonstrated that the most notable winners usually encountered heartbreaking obstacles before they triumphed. They won because they refused to become discouraged by their defeats."

Remember, Success is the progressive realization of worthwhile predetermined, personal goals. Setting goals becomes the mainstay of Renewalment. Wayne Dyer, author and speaker has said, "When I chased after money, I never had enough. When I got my life on purpose and focused on giving of myself and everything that arrived into my life, then I was prosperous."

I promised you the Secret to Life and if you study this and think about it, it will work for you. Remember, we are creatures of habit. Since 95% of everything we do every day is a habit, you need to establish good and positive habits. Here it is. You are what you Think about all day! You are the Sum total of all your thoughts! And the Bible says, "as a Man Thinketh in his Heart (Mind) so is he!" What do you think about all day?

You need to develop PMA. Positive Mental Attitude. You need to read positive books, associate with positive people, be positive all day. Life comes at us fast. Weather, wars, price increases, accidents, hurts and much more. How do you handle each of these situations as they come? With negative thoughts or are you a winner and handle them with positive thoughts? Just remember to have PMA all day long. Positive Mental Attitude.

Join Judy and me in Renewalment and enjoy the rest of your life. Remember EELM. Enjoy Every Luscious Moment.

ISBN 1425179061

9 781425 179069